Lettice

Best Ever Stories

A Christmas Wish
The Flying Rabbit
The Birthday Party

Mandy Stanley

HarperCollins *Children's Books*

Lettice

A Christmas Wish

Lettice Rabbit and her family lived high up
on top of the hill. Nibble, nibble, hop, hop,
every day was the same…

until one cold winter's morning. Lettice peeped out of her burrow to find that the world had turned sparkly white...

'Snow!' squeaked Lettice. 'I've never
seen so much snow.' And she put out
a paw to taste it. But as she leaned out
of her burrow, she slipped...

and tumbled...

over and over...

down towards the pond.

'Heeelp!' shrieked Lettice.

BUMP!
She landed flat on her nose
in the middle of the pond.
It was frozen solid.
As she tried to stand...

she slipped
and skidded...

twizzled and
twirled...

just like an
ice skater.

'Wheee! This is fun,'
Lettice giggled.

Suddenly she stopped.
She could hear voices.

Peeping over the bank, Lettice saw some children. They were having a wonderful time playing in the

snow and collecting things on their toboggan.
'I wonder what they're doing?' thought Lettice.

'Let's go!' called one of the children.
    'Can we finish the Christmas decorations
when we get home?' replied another.

'Christmas!' thought Lettice. 'I've always wanted to know what Christmas is. I'm going to follow them and find out.'

When the children got home they hung
some holly on the front door.

Without them noticing, Lettice slipped
into the house.

Mmm. Something smelled delicious.
   'Biscuits!' yelled the children.
   'But biscuits aren't Christmas,' thought
Lettice, and she hopped into the next
room to explore.

Lettice gasped.

In front of her was a glittering tree, covered with glowing jewels and gold and silver sparkles.

'So *this* is Christmas!' she whispered, hopping closer. Underneath the tree she saw the best thing of all. A gorgeous fairy doll!

Lettice gently took it out of its box.

'I wish *I* could be a fairy!' she sighed.

Just then, the children came into the room…

and happily pulled things out of boxes to put on to the tree.

'But where is the fairy?' said one. 'She's gone!'

'Look what I've found!' said the boy.

'A rabbit!' squealed the children with delight.
'What are you doing here?'

'I just wanted to find out about Christmas,'
blushed Lettice.

'Christmas is about decorating the house and being with the people we love,' said the girl.
'And Father Christmas brings us presents!' said the boy.

'And all our wishes come true,'
said the other little girl.
'I have a Christmas wish,' sighed Lettice.
'I wish I could be a Christmas fairy.'

The children clapped their hands. 'That's easy!'

They made Lettice
a fairy dress,

little sparkly slippers,

and fairy wings made
of tissue and tinsel.

When Lettice saw
her reflection,
she couldn't
believe her eyes.
'I really am a
Christmas fairy.'

Lettice wanted to tell her brothers and sisters all about Christmas.

'We'll take you home on our toboggan,' said the children.

When it was time to say goodbye they gave Lettice a beautiful box.

'Merry Christmas, Lettice!' they cried.

'Oh! Thank you!' cried Lettice and she raced into the burrow.

'Where have you been?' cried all her family.
'I've been to find Christmas,' she said,
opening the box. 'Follow me, I know just
what to do with these!'

Lettice and her brothers and sisters hung the shiny decorations on the tree outside their burrow. The little Christmas tree shimmered and twinkled in the moonlight.

Lettice was so happy, it felt like magic had come to their burrow that night.
'Merry Christmas, everyone,' she called.

Merry Christmas, Lettice.

Lettice

The Flying Rabbit

Lettice Rabbit and her family
lived high up on top of the hill.
Nibble, nibble, hop, hop, every day was the same.
   'Nothing ever happens here,' Lettice sighed,
rolling over on to her back.

Just then a small bird flew overhead.
Lettice watched as it swooped and looped high
over the meadow.

'I wish I could fly,' Lettice thought, 'but it could
only happen in my dreams.'

And Lettice thought how
wonderful it would be to
soar high into the sky, as
light and free as a feather.

'Perhaps I can fly,' thought Lettice.
'I've never even tried.'

Lettice jumped
to her feet.

She flapped her arms,

she flapped her ears.

She even flapped her
whiskers and tail, but
nothing seemed to work.

Lettice flopped down on the grass, very fed up.

'I'll never be able to fly...' suddenly she stopped.
She could hear a strange, deep humming sound.

It was a beautiful pink aeroplane, turning and diving in the sky. 'Wow!' breathed Lettice and she jumped up and scampered after it.

She bounded across the meadow,

under the bramble hedge, over the stile

and through the stream, until, in the
distance, she saw the plane land.

Lettice hopped up to take a closer look. Inside the cockpit was a tiny seat, just the right size for a small rabbit. She *had* to try it.

Lettice wriggled her bottom into the seat.
Suddenly the plane made a loud rumbling
noise. It lurched forward and jolted
up, up, up into the sky.

'Help!'
squealed Lettice.

As she tried to take a peek down below she could see fields and woods stretching far into the distance.

'I never knew the world was this big!' she gasped.

Just then a sudden gust of wind
pushed the little plane sideways.
'Uh, oh!' cried Lettice.

Judder,

Clank,

Whoosh,
went the plane.

And then...

CRASH!

The plane flew into a tree
in the middle of a wood,
a long way from home.

Lettice was thrown out.
She clung on to a branch,
dangling high
above the ground.

'I wish I was safe at home,'
she whispered, tearfully.

Lettice's arms ached and she couldn't
hold on any longer. Her paws slipped
and she began to fall
down

down

down...

...straight into the arms of a little girl.
'What are you doing in my plane?' laughed
the girl, putting her safely on the ground.

'I just wanted to be able
to fly,' sobbed Lettice,
'but it all went wrong and
now I'll never get home.'

'I can fly you back,' said the girl and she showed
Lettice the special control box
that made the plane fly.

'Oh, thank you,' squeaked Lettice. She took a
deep breath and climbed into the seat once again.
The engine started and the plane lifted smoothly
up into the air.

The plane took Lettice high above the wood.
She flew over the fields and river, and then her
very own meadow.

'I love flying!' Lettice squealed as she looped
the loop.

Down below, the Rabbit family looked up, amazed.

'It's Lettice,' they cried. 'Look, she's really flying!'

Once she had landed safely Lettice and her family
bounded back to the burrow.

'We want to fly too!' cried her brothers and sisters,
clapping their paws as Lettice told them her story.

Lettice looked round, thinking she must be the happiest, and luckiest, rabbit in the world.

'Sometimes,' she thought, 'you really can make a dream come true.'

Lettice

The Birthday Party

Lettice Rabbit and her family lived high up on top of a hill. Nibble, nibble, hop, hop, every day was the same, until one afternoon...

Lettice peeped out of the burrow
and saw a little girl with wings,
chasing a balloon.

Lettice scampered after the little girl and
soon she saw a mum and four more children.
'Hello!' said the little girl. 'I'm Jasmine.
It's my birthday party.
Want to join in?'

Lettice didn't need to be asked twice.
She couldn't wait to find out what
happened at a birthday party.

First they played leap frog. Lettice was good at that!

Then they played catch...

...and then
hide and seek.

Next Jasmine opened her birthday presents.
There was a butterfly kite...

a pink
skipping rope,

...and a beautiful princess doll
with lots of different dresses.

But something was
bothering Lettice.

Shyly, she said,
'I wish I had something
special to wear, like you.'

Jasmine held out one of her
doll's dresses. 'You can have this!' she said.
'Can I?' whispered Lettice.

Very carefully,
she stepped into the
tiny dress and shoes.

Jasmine placed a sparkly tiara over
Lettice's ears. It fitted perfectly!
Lettice was a princess!

'Now let's have tea,' said Jasmine's mum.

But, just then, a drop of rain fell on the cake. 'Oh, no!' cried Jasmine. 'It can't rain. Not today!'

'My birthday is *ruined!*' wept Jasmine.
Lettice was upset. What could she do?

Then Lettice
had an idea.

'Come on everyone,
follow me!'
she said.

And she led the way...

...to a beautiful secret glade,
where the trees arched over
and kept out the rain.

It was truly magical.

They lit the candles on the cake
and everyone sang Happy Birthday.

Jasmine blew
out the candles
and made a
secret wish.

After tea, Lettice
peeped outside.
'Look!' she said.
'It's stopped raining.'

Later, on the way home,
they flew the new kite...

...and just as they came to the bottom
of the hill, there was a rainbow.

'Thank you for making this the best
birthday ever!' said Jasmine,
holding out a party bag.
'For me?' blushed Lettice. 'Oh, thank you!'

Lettice waved
goodbye...

...and rushed home to share her
goodies with the family.

The bag was full of pretty things.
Lettice's favourite was a very special balloon.

'Parties are lovely,' sighed Lettice, happily.
'I can't wait for *my* birthday!'

First published in hardback in Great Britain by HarperCollins Children's Books in 2011
First published as *Lettice – A Christmas Wish* in 2003, *Lettice – The Flying Rabbit* in 2002 and *Lettice – The Birthday Party* in 2006

1 3 5 7 9 10 8 6 4 2

ISBN: 978-0-00-790572-0

HarperCollins Children's Books is a division of HarperCollins Publishers Ltd.

Text and illustrations copyright © Mandy Stanley 2002, 2003, 2006

Visit our website at: www.harpercollins.co.uk